The First Easter Bunny

By Frrich Lewandowski

Illustrations by

Anne Schaper Englot

Ambassador Books
Worcester, Massachusetts

The First Easter Bunny

The First Easter Bunny was originally published by Brent Anderson Publishers
First Printing, January 1996
Second Printing, March 1996
Third Printing, February 1997

Revised casebound edition by Ambassador Books, Inc.
First Printing, December 1998
Second Printing, December 2000
Third Printing, December 2001

ISBN: 0-9646439-2-8
Library of Congress Catalog Card Number: 98-74525

Published in the United States by Ambassador Books, Inc.
71 Elm Street, Worcester, Massachusetts 01609
(800) 577-0909

Printed in China.

For current information about all titles from Ambassador Books, visit our website at: www.ambassadorbooks.com

This book is dedicated to my parents, Chet and Ann, who taught me the value of faith and fantasy.

-- Frrich Lewandowski

Other books
by Frrich Lewandowski:

Babci's Angel

 *Shooting Stardust*

It's Christmas Again!

L ong ago,

in a far-off land, there lived a
bunny rabbit who loved to
watch people.

He loved
to watch
people
help
each
other
walk.

He loved to watch people
as they made things from wood
— like tables and chairs.

He loved to watch them bake
breads and cakes.
And he loved the smells that came
from the oven as cookies baked.

He loved to watch
the children play.
They always seemed . . .

. . . so happy and free.

One day people from the town were lining the streets.

The rabbit was excited to see a parade.

The people shouted "Hosanna" as the man rode by on a donkey.

"How exciting," thought the rabbit. "He must be a king or someone very special."

A few days later, there was another parade in town. This time, the rabbit drew a little closer. He saw a man carrying a cross.

The man had a crown of thorns on his head.

This parade sure seemed different from the one a few days earlier.

The rabbit stayed at a safe
distance as he followed along.
Just outside the town, the
parade went up a hill — not too
far from where the rabbit lived.

Then the rabbit saw three crosses being raised. He wanted to get a closer look but waited until most of the crowd had left.

When it seemed safe, the rabbit moved closer. He saw that the man on the cross was the same man who rode the donkey in the parade a few days earlier.

The rabbit was confused, but he remembered how the older rabbits always told the younger rabbits to beware of people because people can change their minds quickly.

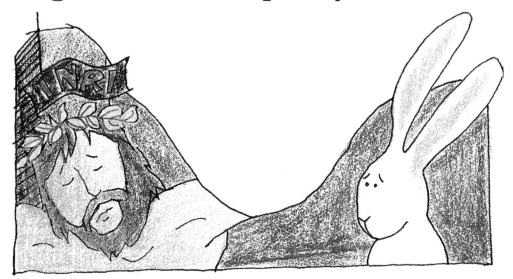

The rabbit looked up at the man.
How sad he looked! How sad too
were his mother and friends who
stood beneath the cross and cried.

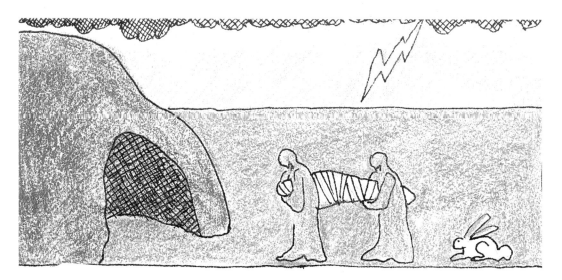

A storm broke out and the rabbit ran —- lightening always frightened him!

From his home, the rabbit saw some people take the man off the cross and place him in a cave.

The rabbit knew what that meant. He had seen other people placed in caves. He knew the man was dead.

A few days later, the rabbit awoke before dawn.

He heard some rumbling and went to investigate.

He walked to the cave where the man was buried. He had entered it many times before. But this morning, a huge stone covered the entrance.

The cave had become a tomb.

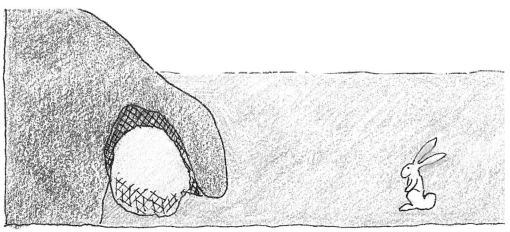

The ground shook and the stone
rolled back and forth until the
entrance to the cave was open
again.

A bright, beautiful light . . .
brighter and more beautiful than
any light the rabbit had ever seen
before . . . filled the cave.

The rabbit went to investigate.
Just as he got to the opening of
the cave, a man started to come
out.

The rabbit looked closely at
the man.

It was the same man he had
seen in the parade a week earlier
--the same man who had hung on
a cross a few days earlier and had
DIED.

Now He was alive!

He was alive!

And the rabbit was the first living creature to see Him.

The rabbit was so excited, he wanted to tell everyone the good news. But he couldn't because rabbits can't talk. He felt so sad and frustrated.

The man bent down and gently patted the rabbit on the back of his neck.

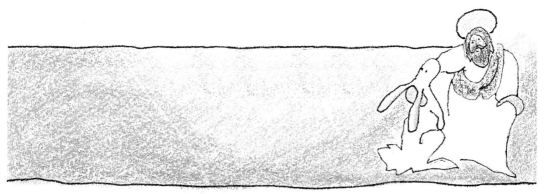

"My little friend," He said, "because you were the first living creature to welcome Me back to life, I want you to bring joy to all the little children who will ever live."

This day will be called 'Easter' and every year on Easter Sunday you will make the little children happy by bringing them sweet treats . . . jelly beans, colored eggs, cookies and cakes."

And for evermore, whenever Easter comes and big people find joy in hearing the good news that Jesus lives, little children will hear that the first living creature to see the Risen Jesus was the

Easter Bunny!